INDEPENDENT LEGIONS PUBLISHING

CHILDREN OF NO ONE

by Nicole Cushing

ISBN: 978-88-99569-69-3
Copyright (Edition) ©2017 Independent Legions Publishing
Copyright (Text) ©2013 Nicole Cushing
1° edition paperback October 2017
Editing: Lucy A. Snyder
Cover Art: bymandesigns
Digital Layout: Lukha B. Kremo

Nicole Cushing

Children
Of No One

To the memory of Sara J. Larson
(1962-2012)

I thought of a labyrinth of labyrinths, of one sinuous spreading labyrinth that would encompass the past and the future and in some way involve the stars.
—*Jorge Luis Borges, "The Garden of Forking Paths"*

As for the quality or characteristic
of unholiness—this is also misleading,
a nominal facade
designed to make things interesting
for a world born out of blackness,
where nothing holy or unholy
has ever existed...
where nothing exists at all
except dreams and fevers
and names for nothing:
the creation, so to speak,
of that original blackness
which pulls itself over every world
like a hangman's hood
over a condemned man's head.

—Thomas Ligotti
"The Name is Nothing" from the poem cycle *The Unholy City*

TWO ARGUING voices echo off the walls of Nowhere, Indiana: the voices of teenage boys, one a tenor who sometimes crosses the border to a baritone, the other a baritone who sometimes crosses the border to a bass. The topic of their current debate: the possible existence of light. There's no evidence of it to be found, at present, but one of them raises the possibility it may have been there, once. A long, long time ago.

"Whoever changed everything oughta get shot," the tenor-baritone says.

"I keep telling you, nothin's *been* changed. Things have always been like this," the baritone-bass replies.

"Bullcrap. Lots has been changed. There's *lots* missing. For starters, I remember *seein'* shit. All kinds of shit, all over the place."

"If you're fixin' to convince me, I suggest you narrow that down a little."

A sigh. "I remember somethin'. Somethin' that used to be around but isn't anymore: low to the ground, long curly hair all over it. Its nose was shaped funny and it had long, floppy ears. I remember it licking me."

"I'm the oldest. If anything like that was ever here, I'd remember it— and I don't."

"Only the oldest by a little, I think."

"So?"

"So maybe you don't remember the light because you don't *want* to remember it. Or maybe you really do remember and just won't say it, because you want to let on that you believe what everyone says, instead of what you know."

"Now listen here, James. That's crazy talk."

"You wanna know what's crazy? The idea that only three things ever existed."

"The dark, the walls, the us. That's it, until we make our way out of here and into Heaven. That's where the light is. The *only* place the light is. You see any evidence to the contrary?"

"Sure. The food."

"Food's just part of us. We take it inside ourselves, dumbass."

"But who brings it out to the Target Zone? Where does it come from?"

"No wonder you got kicked out of school. I reckon you failed your oral exam on the qualities and characteristics of angels. That's, what, fifty percent of your senior year grade?"

"Lookit, it wasn't even a real school. I mean, you *have to* remember what it was like before. We had a real school, before. In the light. There were big people there. Bigger than us, at least. Don't you remember the bigger man who always used to say things like 'bullcrap'? He lived with us."

No reply.

"I mean, you *have to* remember. We made it into first and second grade before all the changes. I remember holding something in my hands. There were flat, thin things that my fingers used to flip through. It was how we learned. There's something wrong with all this. I've always known there's something wrong with all this. The best thing the Tutors ever did is kick me out. Let me go my own way."

"Nope, the best thing that ever happened to you was my decision to let you tag along with me. You'd be dead by now if I hadn't agreed to that."

Then a pause in the debate, as though both voices have come to realize that neither one is en route to convincing the other.

Then the bells ring. Maybe a half dozen of the kind the Angels carry with them. There's a scuffle of feet against dirt, perhaps stirred by a newborn hope. A huff, then grunts. The sound of footsteps moving in the direction of the chimes.

Then the sound of flesh-and-bone colliding with thick oak. A metallic reverberation mixed into the dull thud of wood—as though the boys are living chimes and the walls a maze-shaped bell.

A wail. "Fuckin' walls," the tenor-baritone voice says.

"Fuckin'…What's that word even *mean*?"

"I dunno. I just remember the guy who lived with us used to say that, sometimes, too. It just sounds like it fits this situation."

THE OFFICE wasn't much more than a Quonset hut. Humble, but comfortable. Well-lit. MacPherson asked if he could have a cigarette. Kitterman shrugged and said, "Sure, no smoking bans out here in the country. At least, none that anyone would go through all the trouble to enforce." He put an ashtray embossed with the logo of the Indiana University Hoosiers in between them. Both of them lit up. Kitterman, his Marlboros. Macpherson, his Camels.

Kitterman scratched his neck and scratched his belly (and for all MacPherson knew, scratched his balls under the table with the other hand). He looked twitchy. "So, your flight from, well…wherever it is you flew in from…it go okay?"

Macpherson shrugged and flashed a fake grin. "I'm here, so it could have been worse."

Kitterman wore a pin just over his left shirt pocket. Gold-colored, but probably not gold. An angel. His callused left hand fiddled with it while his right tapped out ashes. "Where'd you fly into? Cincinnati? Indy?"

"Louisville. Weird. You'd figure an old fart like me would have had a firm grasp on geography, but I never noticed Kentucky shared a border with Indiana."

"Yep. Well, here in southern Indiana, I reckon you could say we're *sort* of close to a lot of cities, but not *real* close to any of 'em. Our little town of Nowhere's just less than a two-hour drive from Cincinnati and Indianapolis. How long did it take you from Louisville?"

He looked at his phone. "About ninety minutes. Guess that's why TripAdvisor had me fly into there. Saved time. At least, a little. Got a nice deal on the rental car thanks to AARP. At least I end up getting something out of those membership dues! Take it from me, kid, getting old isn't the worst thing in the world. Not these days." He glanced up to find Kitterman scratching his nose. "Anyway, I've heard you run a hell of a joint here. I look forward to seeing it."

Kitterman ran a hand through his auburn buzz cut and took a deep drag off his cigarette. "Well, that's just the thing. I mean, *ordinarily*, we don't give tours."

MacPherson snorted smoke through his nostrils. "I hope you'll understand that my case is a little out of the ordinary"

"Well, yes, that's why my boss asked me to meet with you. That's why you're here. I have to be honest with you, though. I wouldn't get your hopes up. This…well, this project, likes to keep a low profile."

"You might be surprised by how much I *already know* about your project, Mr. Kitterman. There's gossip afoot among us patrons of the arts. Whispers implying that you and Thomas Krieg have been at this for ten years now. Raising dozens of children in a pitch-black maze. Deciding how much food and water to give them, where to leave it, how to alert them to its presence. Calibrating the environment. Getting the details right. I hope you'll understand that a man in my position doesn't like to be kept waiting to see such a masterpiece."

Kitterman cleared his throat, took another drag of his cigarette, and cleared his throat again. Listened.

"I'm aware Mr. Krieg is a perfectionist," MacPherson said. "Don't get me wrong, I *like* that in an artist. But he needs to be reasonable. He can't keep his fans waiting like this. I think the last time I saw his work was in that Lebanese prison, back in '85. His public has been patient long enough, I think. Don't get me wrong, I admire his fastidiousness. But you should tell Krieg that, at some point, an artist has to stop obsessing over the perfection of his work and put it out there to be enjoyed by the audience."

"Well, my job's the security end of things. I can't say I know a lot about art. But if you were in Lebanon in '85, then you must know how careful we have to be about the authorities. They don't know a lot about art either. I'm sure you've heard all the misunderstandings."

"Ah yes...'Krieg the Torturer'... 'Krieg the Sadist.' Honestly, I can't say for certain that these are misunderstandings. I happen to think these characterizations are spot on."

Kitterman let out a series of spastic coughs, then crumbled what was left of his cigarette into the ashtray. "I, I see."

"I hope this doesn't bore you. But maybe if I share with you my perspective on all of this, it'll reassure you as to my sincerity. You see, I've always been an admirer of performance art— or as I like to think of it, *behavioral* art.

That's why Krieg's work is right up my alley. When I was just an undergrad at NYU, I took in a show Yoko Ono gave. 'Cut Piece.' Have you heard of it?"

"Like I said, sir, the art isn't really my end of things..."

"Well, let me describe it to you." Kitterman didn't look enthusiastic about being on the receiving end of such an explanation, but didn't interrupt.

"You see, in 'Cut Piece,' Ono sat on the stage wearing a black dress. A pair of scissors lay on stage next to her. She invited members of the audience to come up and cut pieces of her dress off. When there was no more dress, she invited audience members to cut off her slip...her bra, her panties, even. Until there was nothing left. Or until she decided the show was over. It was personal violation as art, you see. Yoko Ono and Thomas Krieg know the same thing: that sometimes art depends on humiliation. Or, *hell*, take Picasso's *Guernica*.

15

Sometimes art depends on death, mutilation. If the fascists hadn't bombed some Basques in 1937, we wouldn't have that magnificent work of art. I approach your black maze of Nowhere, Indiana, very much in the same spirit as I would either of these two works."

Kitterman scratched his neck. Then, for the first time during this meeting, he looked MacPherson in the eyes. "I can see you're enthusiastic about all of this. And serious about this. That's good news for you. I hope you'll understand that Mr. Krieg will require you to undergo a few background checks before we'll grant you permission to view the piece. For starters, we'll need to verify your statement that you were in the audience in that Lebanese prison in '85."

"Verify?"

"You're not the only one with means, sir. If you attended the performance in Lebanon, we should still have the records. A precaution, you understand. We don't like the idea of audience members enjoying the show, but then finding themselves afflicted with a bad case of scruples after it's all over and providing anonymous tips to unfriendly branches of the government. By keeping thorough records of everyone who attends our shows, we protect ourselves. If Krieg goes down, then the audience goes down, too."

MacPherson took a deep drag of his Camel. "May I confess something to you, Mr. Kitterman? That excitement, the underground ambiance, the risk...that's all part of the reason I flew all the way out here to Bum Fuck, Indiana—no offense."

"None taken. Now, like I said, we'll be performing our background checks. Perusing our old records. I'll just need to get a photo of you now, so we can compare it to the one from Lebanon and make sure they reasonably match."

"It's been almost thirty years."

"No worries, we have experts for that sort of thing. Top people." He pulled a camera out of his drawer, asked MacPherson to sit still, and snapped three shots from various angles. "We'll also need you to sign a temporary power of attorney form granting us full access to your bank account."

"I beg your pardon?"

Kitterman sighed. "I'm sure you'll understand. We need confirmation—unfortunately, above and beyond your own word—that you can afford the experience. More importantly, we need confirmation that your financial transactions aren't vulnerable to investigation. I hope you'll understand our position on the matter. No one has ever been granted permission to observe a Krieg piece while it's still in the process of being assembled. You'd be the first. Unique opportunities require unique security precautions. Surely a man of your position can understand."

MacPherson bit his lower lip. Stamped his cigarette out in the ashtray. Leaned back. Crossed his arms. "Give me twenty-four hours to think about it. That's reasonable, isn't it?"

Kitterman shook his head, then scratched it. "That just

won't do. Mr. Krieg is a man of little patience. A visitor on site will mean many complications to his daily routine, which he insists on knowing about as soon as possible. I, well, I'm sorry but I've been instructed to give you twenty-four *minutes.* You can think about it out in the waiting area. I suggest you not discuss it any further and get to mulling over your pros and cons."

MacPherson rose from his seat, lit a fresh Camel, and didn't so much walk as *stagger* toward the front of the Quonset hut, to a love seat and coffee table that alone comprised what Kitterman had so generously dubbed a "waiting area." He accepted that, as an artist, Krieg had a bit of an eccentric, self-indulgent streak. But this really was going too far.

Still, he didn't leave the Quonset hut immediately. He sat there and stewed. He'd traveled relatively far. He'd just gotten there. To leave immediately would prove anticlimactic. Perhaps the security man was being overly literal in his interpretation of one of Krieg's commands. Perhaps Krieg could be persuaded that what he was asking for exceeded good common sense.

He stubbed out his cigarette and went to find Krieg's guard dog to convince him that something had gotten lost in translation, but when he took his first step, he became dizzy. He wobbled backward, flailed for something to hold on to.

The world first turned black, then turned cold, then turned velvet. He collapsed into a seat. It wasn't the love seat in the Quonset hut. It was a front-row aisle seat in what appeared to be a gaudy old theater of the rococo variety. He craned his head to see what appeared to be a performance in progress. A glaring spotlight lingered atop a trembling emaciated teenage boy seated on the middle of the stage, in a wooden chair. The teenager wore what seemed to be the ragged remains of blue jeans and a T-shirt, but had no shoes. His hair was a long, unkempt rat's nest. MacPherson noted the boy's long, chipped fingernails and toenails.

MacPherson struggled to find words to describe the next character to appear. It was, perhaps, a person covered head to toe in loose black fabric. He saw no opening in the fabric through which an actor could have seen or spoken or breathed.

A pair of scissors lay on the stage. The Thing in Black picked them up with what seemed to be a hand and placed one of the boy's fingers in-between the blades.

The boy didn't move. The finger fell away like hair from a barber's shears. The Thing in Black picked it up with what seemed to be a hand and fed it into what seemed to be a mouth. Then the spotlight followed the Thing in Black as it sauntered away from the boy and the chair, stage left. An antique microphone awaited it there. It pointed at MacPherson.

"You're the first one in the theater," the Thing in Black said in a voice that seemed to be MacPherson's own.

MacPherson looked down the front row, then across the

19

aisle, then behind him and verified the Thing was correct.

"But if you say no to Kitterman, then Krieg will invite others. And then you'll have lost out on your chance. If you don't sign those papers, another patron of the arts will. You don't want *that,* do you?"

MacPherson shook his head to indicate to the Thing that, no, he would definitely *not* want that.

"But if you sign them, then…I promise you…you won't regret it."

Then MacPherson wasn't in his cushy velvet seat at all, but was instead on stage and in the spotlight. Tucked inside black fabric. Or, perhaps he wasn't tucked inside anything at all. Maybe he *was* black fabric. Black fabric that held scissors in something like a hand, and took them to the trembling boy's left ear. Black fabric that hesitated one exquisite moment to savor its robust power and the boy's corresponding frailty.

Snip!

Kitterman shook his head, then scratched it. "That just won't do. Mr. Krieg is a man of little patience. A visitor on site will mean many complications to his daily routine, which he insists on knowing about as soon as possible. I, well, I'm sorry but I've been instructed to give you twenty-four *minutes.* You can think about it out in the waiting area. I suggest you not discuss it any further and get to mulling over your pros and cons."

MacPherson found himself back in the Quonset hut, and

somehow five minutes back in time. No sign of the stage or the spotlight. He wiped sweat off his brow. His heart fluttered. He stammered. "I, I th-think we can work something out along those lines. Allow me to make a few calls."

"Twenty-four minutes, starting now. Mr. Krieg's specific instructions. I'm sure you'll understand that that's why I have to remain rather firm on the matter. Krieg doesn't pay me to be flexible."

In the next twenty-four minutes many phone calls ensued from MacPherson to his subordinates, tax attorneys, and stock brokers. Demands to know if there was anything shady to be concerned about. They mentioned one or two small things— matters easily enough withdrawn from for the sake of Experience. He commanded his broker to make the necessary sales (at a loss, to avoid accusations of guilt). He commanded his lawyer to refrain from writing off some expenses that might have proven difficult to justify. It would mean a seven-figure hit from the tax man, but well worth the insights into Krieg's method he'd be granted by the agreement. Well worth the apex of Behavioral Art. The suffering children—how he *yearned* to see them outside of his daydreams.

The decision made, the paperwork followed. Page after page in need of a signature that MacPherson was only too eager to offer. He didn't read any of the forms in their entirety. He skimmed.

"Very well," Kitterman said. "When would you like to meet

Mr. Krieg? When do you fly back?"

"Well, I, I hadn't booked a flight back yet. I wanted to see how matters here proceeded, you see. When might he be available?"

"I'll tell you what: why don't you go ahead and get yourself a room back in town. There's an inn on Mulberry that business travelers—the few we get up around these parts, anyway—use when they're here. They're never fully booked, and it's pleasant enough accommodations. Get some rest, and I'll let Mr. Krieg know you've agreed to the terms. We'll review your background check and be in touch in the next few days to determine the best time to commence your experience."

Two NOISES: the ringing of bells and the growling of stomachs; the latter superimposed upon the former. Then a third sound: that of a palm smacking a wall. Intentionally. Violently. The slap echoes throughout hundreds of feet of Nowhere, Indiana.

Then a voice—that of the younger of the two young men. "Maybe there's a tiny passage through here. Maybe that's the way to get closer to the food drop."

"Fuck...we're no closer to the manna than we were yesterday. We must be going in circles."

And the bells keep clanging, telling the brothers they still have time to be fed by the Angels—all they need to do is negotiate the twists and turns. All they have to do is feel their way around until they reach the right alcove of Nowhere—the place where the Angels ring bells and give out food. The place where they and all the other boys from Nowhere gather and trade war stories about the misery they went through to arrive at the bells. The place in which they swap survival tips, and sleep. (Oh how deeply they sleep, even though they pass out amidst the chiming of the bells. Oh how they dread waking up to silence because that means the Angels have moved farther on into Nowhere; someplace so far away they can't even be heard.)

THE CALL came much earlier than expected—that very night at 12:46 a.m. MacPherson almost missed it because his phone merely vibrated vigorously against the hotel's nightstand rather than lighting up and ringing. Had he been so careless as to put it on the wrong setting at such an important time?

The voice on the other end of the phone had a British accent. "Mac*Pher*-son?"

"Sp-speaking."

"Mistah Krieg asked me to give you a call to officially welcome you to Nowhere!"

MacPherson found this to be a gaffe on the Englishman's part. Technically speaking, he wasn't yet in Nowhere. Nowhere, Indiana, was the art installation...somewhere underground, somewhere near the Quonset hut. This was the town next to Nowhere. (What was it called? Madison? Mason?) Surely, the

Englishman knew this? Perhaps he merely meant to welcome him to the *Experience* of Nowhere, rather than the *place*."

"Why...why thank you. I have to admit, I didn't expect to hear from anyone else associated with Krieg until tomorrow, at the earliest."

"Tut, tut, Mr. Mac-*Pher*-son. Look at the date on your cell phone. It *is* tomorrow."

"Well, you know, I meant daylight."

"Daylight's overrated. Each day begins anew at midnight. Curious, eh? Perhaps an unconscious recognition on the part of civilization that darkness is at the 'eart of things. What do we see outside our windows the very first moment of a new day? Darkness. What do we see the very last moment of a day soon to pass? Darkness. Mankind could 'ave just as easily set each day to roll into another at noon, but chose not to. Tacit acknowledgement, I think, that Darkness is the alpha and the omega. In the beginning and, most especially at the end, that's all there is."

MacPherson had never before heard such an argument (and he'd thought he'd heard it all). The novelty was intoxicating. At that moment, he felt reassured that he'd made the right decision in agreeing to Krieg's terms.

"In any event," the Englishman continued. "Mistah Krieg 'as prepared a new exhibit, specifically for *your* appreciation. A new Experience, you might say. Set to commence immediately. Meet us in the alley next to the inn."

24

"So my background check has been approved? Already?"

"We'll discuss the matter of your background check in a few moments, Mistah Mac-*Pher*-son. Mistah Krieg would prefer to discuss it face-to-face."

MacPherson coughed. Felt a sense of unease crawl over him like ants. Had Kitterman found something, already, that would endanger his Experience? He wanted answers now, but feared ticking off Krieg's henchman. "Why, yes, of course. Now, if you could just allow me to take a shower—"

"That won't be necessary," the Englishman sniped. "If you'll pardon the egregious pun, Mistah Krieg is quite literally an underground artist. Body odor goes with the territory of working sixteen hours a day in a subterranean bunker. If 'e doesn't care ow 'e smells, why on earth should 'e care about *your* odor?"

"U-understandable," MacPherson stammered. "Then I'll be down just as soon as I can put on some clothes."

"Mistah Krieg says the briefing starts in five minutes. If you're serious about this, you'll be down here in three. Starting...now."

MacPherson dispatched with any formality whatsoever. The only things he bothered to don for the occasion were socks and shoes. He'd neglected to pack sneakers, and so he slipped on black socks and penny loafers instead. Combined with his sweatpants, T-shirt, and beard stubble they created a garish ensemble. He glanced in the full-length mirror that hung in his room and cringed, noticing he looked like a derelict. He grabbed his room key and wallet and slipped out the door.

No time to wait for an elevator. He took the stairs instead. His shoes made conspicuous clip-clop sounds and the night clerk looked up from the smart phone on which she'd been texting and eyed him suspiciously.

"It's me," MacPherson said. "The guest in room 312. Just going out for a bit."

She gave him a puzzled look. He feared she thought him a trespassing vagrant. Moments passed, then finally a glint of recognition. "Oh yes," she said, perhaps remembering some distinguishing mark in his generally unremarkable face, or, more likely, picking up a clue from his voice. "Going out to see the eclipse?"

"Just going for a walk," he said. He wasn't the sort of person who kept close tabs on the movements of heavenly bodies. He couldn't remember the last time he'd seen a lunar eclipse. High school? Some other time in his life, he wagered, back before he worked twenty hours a day and slept only four.

He took on a brisker pace, and soon enough found himself in the cool night air. Although the quaint small-town road was well-populated with street lamps, only a few provided illumination of any sort (and even these flickered on and off, faintly, like strobe lights.) He turned left out the front door of the hotel and made another left into the alley.

Two men stood in silhouette, one shorter than the other.

The taller one held a crowbar. Alongside them, steam drifted up from the asphalt. Then something at their feet. A heavy-looking metal disk. They'd just removed a manhole cover from its moorings.

The short man walked forward, out of the shadows and into the faint, shredded light that made its way into the alley. He wore a Fu Manchu mustache, a leather jacket, and a red beret pierced with various and sundry pins. He looked at a pocket watch. "Just barely in time." A nondescript American voice. He placed the watch into an inside pocket of his jacket and clapped one black-gloved hand against another in slow, ironic applause.

The tall man was the Englishman. "Shall we take 'im down now?"

"Yes, let's." He then turned to address MacPherson directly. "I wish I could say I was taking you down the rabbit hole. Alas, a *man*hole will have to suffice."

MacPherson approached the cavity in the ground with some trepidation. He couldn't see how he could safely take the plunge.

"There's a ladder," the Englishman said. "'unch down this way. I'll show you." MacPherson felt a huge, callused paw suddenly grasp his own trembling hand, guiding it downward until he felt the touch of rusty metal. He then reached out his other hand and found the other rail. He put his leg down, tentatively searching for the first step. Finding it, he started his descent. As he began to go down, he craned his head skyward. Overhead, he spied the full moon. The eclipse-in-progress stained it with shades of red and black. It looked bruised, but still shining.

"Pretty now, ain't it?" the Englishman said. "But if you wanted to see the eclipse, you could 'ave just gone to an observatory. C'mon now, get a move on."

And so he did.

He clung close to the bottom of the ladder while the other two men worked their way down. The Englishman dragged the cover back over top of the hole with one hand and carried the crowbar back down with him.

"Stay close," Krieg said. "Just follow us." MacPherson kept up with the men through twists and turns, around and around the sewer and cistern. Krieg and the Englishman seemed to navigate their surroundings by touch. It was as though they'd memorized the tactile sensations of each inch of cement, each pipe, each bit of grime, and used them as landmarks.

The group stopped. MacPherson heard a metal door slide open. Then light. Shocking illumination, sufficient—it seemed—to scald his eyes. The men dragged him through the opening. The Englishman tossed the crowbar down to the cement floor with a clang and put on a pair of sunglasses he'd had tucked away in his jacket. Krieg donned sunglasses, too. MacPherson had none. He could only cover his eyes with his hands and peek in between his fingers.

Krieg walked toward a far wall on the other side of the room. "You'll want to come over here, MacPherson, this is the art I wanted to show you."

The Englishman lingered near the tourist.

"And m-my background check," MacPherson stammered. "We'll talk about that?"

"Indeed," the Englishman said. He nudged MacPherson. Gently grasped MacPherson's hands and pried them off his face. Put something plastic into them. Sunglasses. "There," he said. "Don't say I never did anything for you." He let out a hoarse laugh.

MacPherson put on the sunglasses and found his environs— for the first time in what seemed far too long—acceptably lit. Neither too bright nor too dark. For the first time, he caught a full glimpse of the Englishman, and found him to be a hairy, bony, demented-looking nightmare of a man. Not an inch of his face was left uncovered by beard, ink, or piercing.

The tattoos—odd, sinister symbols, perhaps pictographs from languages long expelled from the Earth by a merciful God. A long, scraggly mane framed that desecrated face.

MacPherson grudgingly followed the Englishman, joining Krieg at the wall. The artist was admiring a series of documents and black-and-white photographs—dozens of them—framed side by side, row after row. MacPherson approached and, in a matter of moments, became aware that all the framed pictures were of him, and that all the framed consent forms bore his signature. In the photos, he appeared vaguely desperate. Each signature looked rushed. A flat-screen television hung above all the framed papers and pictures. It was playing what seemed to be a surveillance tape of his meeting with Kitterman.

Krieg smiled, showing crooked, decaying teeth. "I've titled this exhibit 'The Yearning.' Surely you'd agree that's appropriate, wouldn't you, Mr. MacPherson. This piece—or rather, *set* of pieces—captures, quite visually, the desperate desire you have to know my work from the inside out."

"Mistah Krieg likes to play practical jokes. Most of the time they're lame, but this one..." The Englishman placed his hand over his mouth to suppress a giggle. Then he looked up at MacPherson with faux-earnest eyes. "I 'eard someone once say that art sometimes depended on 'umiliation. Do you think that's right, Mistah MacPherson?"

MacPherson gritted his teeth. Considered his options. Decided to play along and offered a fake laugh to join in with the Englishman. "Okay," he conceded. "You got me."

He thought about the hit he'd taken on some of the transactions. Seven figures. Gritted his teeth again. "I can take a joke. It's easy for you to make fun, Krieg. You're the artist. You don't appreciate just how unique your work is, because it's the work you live with, twenty-four/seven. I can understand how my 'yearning' could seem so fanatical as to lead you to ridicule me." The wheels in his brain kept turning. If it was all a game, then perhaps he could make a few phone calls. Reverse course. Prevent at least some of the losses he'd only too eagerly agreed to take. "So, you plan to use none of the documents I've signed? They're to remain up here, as a testament of my fanaticism?"

"Perhaps," said Krieg. "I haven't decided yet. I'm tempted to take them off the wall and have my man on the surface exercise the power of attorney to redirect wealth from your accounts to ours." He waved a hand toward the framed documents. "After all, how much can your money mean to you if you'd put it all at risk for Experience? For, as you like to put it, behavioral art?"

MacPherson felt his pride shrivel inside of him like rotting fruit. "Money is only a means to an end. That's true enough. Art is what makes a man feel truly alive, but I'd appreciate it if you kept your word and only used them for background checks. Anyway, I did what you asked me to do. I've lived up to my end of the bargain. Do you plan to live up to yours?"

The Englishman snickered. "Do you 'ear 'im questioning your integrity, Mistah Krieg? Are you gonna stand for that?"

Krieg smirked. "He's just nervous, that's all. On the one hand, he's unable to stand still, because he's so excited about his impending Experience. On the other, he's terrified at the financial sacrifice he's made as his part of the exchange. He's terrified because he's never had to make hard choices—not *really* hard choices."

MacPherson didn't like Krieg and the Englishman talking about him this way. Like he wasn't even there. "The Art, Krieg. Now. I want explanations. I want details. I want to see Nowhere."

Krieg turned to him. "And see it you shall! But first, follow us into the briefing room. More will be revealed!"

"I FEEL the vibrations from the bells on the walls now," the younger boy says.

"You *better* be telling the truth," the older one says. "I don't want any lies that just make me feel better."

The younger boy laughs. "But that's all you do. Lie to yourself about all this. Pretend you don't remember the light."

A slap. The younger boy cries out. The older boy starts lecturing. "You think the Angels give out food to those who claim light exists anywhere other than Heaven? You think the Angels take kindly to blasphemers?"

The younger boy screams. "There *was* light somewhere else! I saw it. It was—"

The sound of a body getting shoved against the wall. Then words not so much said, but hissed. "Shut up! You don't remember nothing... okay? Can we agree on that, at least until we find the next manna drop?"

"It's not manna it's—"

The sound of flesh pounded. A ragged growl resolving itself into another "Shut up!" and then the sound of a body hitting the floor, and the sound of skin tearing. There, in a corridor of Nowhere, Indiana—where no dogs or birds or airplanes distract the ear from the sounds of human violence—the sound of skin tearing is not only audible but distinctive. Like a hiss. Like a zipper.

More sounds of the older boy lecturing. "No more words about light! No more doubting what we were taught! Understood? Are you trying to make things worse? You want them to punish us?"

"B-but it's not r-right…"

The older boy makes a sound like barking. It's half growl, half grunt. There's a tussle. Then, for a moment, nothing. Silence. Then shrieks.

Frantic, crazed shrieks as the Doppler effect takes hold of their voices—as the sounds sink into the maw of the ground that has just swallowed them up.

KRIEG, THE Englishman, and MacPherson sat in the conference room in the sewers. The Englishman poured hot water out of a kettle into three mugs with waiting bags of Earl Grey. "We might 'ave to keep things simple down 'ere, but we don't 'ave to live like barbarians. This 'ere's fresh, siphoned off from the 'otel."

"I see… so this area down here… around the sewers…it's connected to the inn…does it somehow…well… *connect* to Nowhere?"

"Nowhere is a series of underground tunnels out in the country," Krieg said. "This...office... is very purposefully *unconnected* to Nowhere."

"What Mistah Krieg means to say is, this is the *real* bunkah. The War Room. Just like Adolph 'itlah 'ad. If there's ever an emergency in Nowhere, this is a place we can all lay low but stay close by."

Krieg leaned back in his chair and put his feet up on the table. "Hitler. Really? What a flattering comparison. I guess that would make you, with your lovely long tresses, my Eva Braun?"

The Englishman whipped his tongue out and licked his own mustache, beard, and piercings. "I'm not just a pretty face," he said. "I'm power 'ungry, too. More Eva Perón than Eva Braun."

Krieg giggled. "Well, what do you think of the way my second-in-command flaunts his ambitions, MacPherson?"

"I'd say that's truth in advertising. Honesty's a rarity, these days, and good help is hard to find. I'd hang on to him."

Krieg stroked his chin. "Or... maybe...just plain *hang* him! What would you think of that, Mr. MacPherson? Would you enjoy the Experience of lynching a Brit down in the deepest bowels of Nowhere? Would *that* suit your aesthetic sense?" He reared his head back and let out a cackle. "Can you imagine the sight of those poor idiot redneck bastards stumbling around in the dark until they find *this* stinking Limey's even-stinkier-than-usual *corpse* hanging from the ceiling?"

The Englishman chuckled. "Those feral brats? They'd probably eat me. At least then I'd know my death wouldn't be in vain. I'd probably feed a whole gaggle of your Wild Children of Darkness for a few days. I guess you'd say that'd make me an Angel, in a manner of speakin', now wouldn't it? An' if you don't mind me sayin' so, Mistah Krieg, I'd probably feed twice as many whelps as your scrawny arse could."

Krieg turned to MacPherson. "Such quick wit...you see why I keep him around? He gets my sense of humor."

MacPherson let out a titter. He instinctively reached toward his T-shirt's breast pocket, looking for his Camels. Soon enough he realized he hadn't had time to bring them down with him. He fidgeted in his chair. "So this is your assistant. What, exactly, does he assist you with?"

"Please...Mistah Krieg is an artist, not some sort of mad scientist from a 1940s 'orror show. Mad scientists 'ave 'assistants'. Artists 'ave 'students'...and 'collaborators'—I prefer to think of meself as the latter. I'm not 'ere to learn from Mistah Krieg, as 'e an' I have great differences of opinion on the nature of art. But that doesn't mean we can't work together— that 'is work can't enrich mine and vicey-versa."

MacPherson nodded. Excited, finally, to move past the bullshit and onward into discussing the meat of the matter— onward into discussing just how Nowhere worked. "Do you have paper?" he asked. "If possible, I'd like to take notes."

"No notes," Krieg said. "I've no way to guarantee you

wouldn't misquote me."

MacPherson sighed. "Very well, then. Can you ι explain to me how Nowhere works? What's the divis.ᵗᵗ labor between you, Mr. Krieg, and...well, I'm sorry...I ι caught the name of this other gentleman..."

"I don't 'ave a name."

"Beg your pardon?"

"A name..." the Englishman said. "I said I don't 'ave one. You see, names imply fixed *identity*. If I were to use a name, I would be succumbing to the delusion that there is a real personality—something like a soul—lurking somewhere inside...hiding amid me blood an' gore an' nerves an' sinew. I 'appen to know I'm just a sack of mobile meat. 'Owever, if you *do* feel compelled to refer to me in the course of conversation, you should know I answer to the appellation 'No One.'"

Krieg rolled his eyes. "Don't get him started, MacPherson. The big galoot is pleasant enough to hang out with until you get him started on that nihilist crap."

Mr. No One looked at MacPherson and sneered. "And Mistah Krieg is a nice enough bloke until you get 'im started on that sadist crap."

Krieg shrugged. Took his feet off the table. "I'm not a sadist, I'm just an artist who wants to provoke the strongest possible reaction from his audience. And what provokes a stronger reaction than observing another person suffer?

There's a demand to watch people suffer, because suffering is the foundation of all great drama... all great art. This was true even going as far back as those poor, poor dead children in *Medea*. The human species has an inherent *yearning* to watch its members suffer. Always has, always will. If I didn't work to meet this demand, someone else would."

Mr. No One spread his long arms over the table and leaned forward.

"So, what you're saying is that you're a sadist, but only because market forces compel you in that direction? 'Ow...American."

Krieg sighed, deep and dramatically. "Okay...*just for the sake of argument*, let's say I really am this big, mean ol' sadist you portray me as. At least sadism *sells*."

"Such a *commercial* approach. There's that 'pop art' influence again," Mr. No One said. He turned to MacPherson. "Did you ever 'ear where Mistah Krieg got 'is idea for the lovely black underground maze you'll be seein' la'er today? Ya ever 'ear who's the true Father of Nowhere?"

MacPherson shook his head.

"Andy...Fucking...Warhol. True story."

"What the fu—"

Krieg interrupted. "I knew him, back in the days before I changed direction. This goes all the way back before Beirut, if you want to know the truth. Once, at a party—while under the influence of a wee bit too much blow—I boasted that I could sell a totally black canvas and some poor dupe in Manhattan would buy it. Andy said he'd take me up on that bet, as long as I could make a *sincere* argument to him about why the art had any value...about why it *interested me*. I ended up taking a totally new direction with things, with my work in Lebanon...moving into performance art rather than painting. And then Andy died, of course, but his bet about the black canvas still haunted me."

"So," MacPherson said, "Nowhere, Indiana, is your black canvas?"

"Precisely. The way to make a black canvas interesting is to give it three dimensions, and animate it with human behavior! *Behavior* becomes the artistic medium."

"How did you get the kids? I mean, just logistically, that had to be a challenge. Prisoners in Beirut are one thing—it had to be comparatively easy to acquire them and get the rights to work in the prison. But using *children...American* children as your medium, right here *in* America...much harder, I'd imagine."

"That's the best part, MacPherson. Those particular art supplies were obtained fair and square. The parents were well-reimbursed for my rights to use their children. I used the proceeds from the Lebanon show to help fund the project. I had to be careful, of course. Just one or two at a time... plucked from the poorest areas of the Rustbelt Midwest—not just Indiana, mind you. You see, poor children are so much more dispensable—both to society and to their families. While driving through town, did you notice any of the families? Two, three, four kids hanging off a doped-up single mom? The poor, like deer, tend to over-reproduce. In that way, a life in Nowhere might actually be more merciful to these children than life outside of Nowhere. After all...they get food—all they have to do is find it. And the clever ones, the strong ones, *will* find it. Yes, I give them food and I give them *hope*. Did you know, MacPherson, they believe in Angels? That's who we've taught them brings the food. We've made them believe in manna. That's what they call the food. We've made them believe in Heaven. That's where they believe the Angels come from. That's the only place they think light exists. I've given them *faith*, MacPherson. *Unshakable* faith. I'm protecting them from all the outside forces in the world that would *rob* them of faith."

"But..." MacPherson said weakly, as though reluctant to press the matter, but being unable to help himself, "...some of them surely do die."

Mr. No One smirked. "Some of 'em starve. Some of 'em stop trying to find the food, 'uddle in a corner, in the fetal position, and stay there until they die rather than continue in the maze. Some of 'em seem to tear their own skin to pieces with their nails. Some of 'em seem to be torn apart by others of 'em. Some of 'em..."

Krieg grimaced. "You've made your *point*, No One."

"But 'e's *not* a *sadist*. Yes, let's make that quite clear now, shall we? Mistah Krieg is *not* a sadist."

"Say what you will about sadism," MacPherson said. "At least no one can call it boring."

"Listen 'ere, Fancy-Pants. One shouldn't adopt a philosophy based on 'ow *exciting* one finds it."

"Does sadism qualify as a philosophy?" MacPherson countered. "Isn't it more of an aesthetic? Á la Bosch?"

Mr. No One shook his head. "Aesthetics are a distraction. *Blackness* is the alpha and the omega. That's the important thing."

MacPherson cleared his throat. "So, um, Mr. No One, if you're not crazy about Mr. Krieg's use of the children, why do you bother helping him? Why put yourself at risk for something you don't believe in?"

"Don't get me wrong," Mr. No One said. "I *believe in* Nowhere because I believe in Blackness. I believe I *am* Blackness. I believe the greatest gift I can give me species is to remove the gaudily painted funeral shroud away from the corpse of the stillborn/ever-decaying universe, point to it, and tell everyone to take a big sniff and smell the rot!"

"What's that have to do with Nowhere?"

"I'm a magician," Mr. No One said.

Krieg threw up his hands and giggled. "He's mental."

"It saddens me," Mr. No One said, "that Mistah Krieg isn't better informed about 'is field. A wise, old magician back 'ome once explained it to me this way: back in ancient times, magick and art were one and the same. This fellow, 'e said that if you look back at early tomes on the subject of sorcery, they refer to magick as 'the art' and that this is to be taken quite literally: art is magick and magick is art. Magick and writing are even *more* specifically tied to each other. 'To cast a spell' just means 'to spell.' A 'grimoire' is just an old way of saying 'grammar.' In any event, I believe Nowhere 'as quite a bit more potential than Mistah Krieg could ever imagine. You see, I believe Nowhere, Indiana, can serve as a sort of *battery* for a magickal engine that will remove the gimcrack tarp from the universe and reveal the beautiful black nothing underneath. All I need to do is perform the proper ceremony to invoke the Great Dark Mouth, to invite it to come and gobble up our tacky delusions of light, life and meaning. I came to Nowhere with the specific agenda of elevating it from soft-core torture porn to *ritual*, and tonight—with the added power of the eclipse—that is exactly what I'll do."

"That's why he insisted I take you up on your request to observe Nowhere, MacPherson."

"For art and, consequently, magick to work, it needs an audience. Art isn't art without it."

"I went ahead and humored him. I think it'll be a *gas* when it gets to be the darkest part of night and he goes into the corridors of Nowhere, and says his magic words, and they merely echo back to him emptily."

41

"If I attempted the ritual earlier during my stay in Nowhere, then I'm sure that's just what would have 'appened. But I've convinced Mistah Krieg to make certain *enhancements* that raised this project's magickal power exponentially."

"I was fine with them. The ideas seemed interesting enough, and No One bankrolled the whole thing from his trust fund. It would appear that No One's grandfather was quite a Some One."

"That joke was funny the first ten times you told it," Mr. No One said. "Now it's just stale—like your approach to art. Anyway, Mac*Pher*son, what I did 'ere, I revolutionized Mistah Krieg's maze. Made it more complex."

"Now see," MacPherson said, "*this* is the sort of detail I'd like to get my hands on. Before I go and take a look at Nowhere, I'd like to see a map. If I'm to be the first audience member to enjoy this exhibition, I must have access to a *guidebook,* just so I can find my way around the place."

Mr. No One snickered. "Sorry, chap, but there's no such thing as a *guide* to Nowhere, Indiana. You see, one of the innovations I've introduced is the twenty-four/seven work crew."

MacPherson frowned. "Beg pardon?"

"The maze is constantly changing," Krieg said. "No One suggested the idea, and I liked it because I thought it'd bedevil the little guttersnipes, so I let him implement it. I've hired a handful of art students—devotees to my kind of work—to go down there and rearrange things each and every day. Some days they're erecting walls where walls never before stood. Other days they're tearing walls down and creating new paths."

"But always," No One said, "always, they are commanded to grow the thing outward. To always expand. You see, that way, Nowhere is like *a living creatcha*. The tunnels always writhing in new directions."

"This way, the frustration of the children is always fresh," Krieg said. "They can never learn the right way around, because Nowhere becomes ever more complex each day...but because they'll follow the bells to reach the food they'll always push forward."

This description of the project took MacPherson's breath away. Krieg (or, more rightly said, his collaborator) had managed to impress him. "This just sounds"—he felt a shiver up his back— "delightful."

"You haven't even 'eard the best of it," Mr. No One said. "You see, back when Mistah Krieg was doing this project without a magician's consultation, he had the kiddies only moving in two directions. Forward/backward. Left/right. I mean, 'Zzzzzzz!', right? *I'm* the one who came up with the notion of introducing pitfalls and 'oles in the ceiling, as it were. Just in the last day or two, thanks to me input, Nowhere is now three-dimensional!"

WHEN THE boys land after plummeting down the hole, there's a collage of sound: two six-foot slaps onto the ground, a noise somewhere in between the snap of a tree branch and the crunch of breaking brick, the sound of air puffing out of lips, and—from the younger of the two—wailing, ever more wailing.

"Fuck!" the youngster says. "That hole swallowed us up!"

At this point, one might expect to hear the baritone-bass voice start ranting about how they've been cast down into even deeper bowels of the earth by angry Angels who are punishing them for entertaining blasphemy. But the only voice is the younger brother's.

"Hey!" he hollers. "Are you okay?"

No response.

Up, up, far overhead rings the distant chime of Angels' bells.

WHEN MACPHERSON ascended the ladder, the eclipse was no longer straight overhead, but had veered off to his left, toward the horizon. Rust-colored light stained the scattered clouds like blood leaking through a bandage. The English fiend replaced the manhole cover. Krieg cracked his knuckles. "*Now* we're ready to take you to Nowhere. Excited, MacPherson?"

"Intrigued," MacPherson said, trying to contain himself.

"Pshaw," Mr. No One said. "I think 'e just got an erection." Then belly laughs, deep and haughty, as No One pressed the button on his key that remotely unlocked his Humvee. A vanity plate adorned the rear: IAMNO1. The men piled into the vehicle. Mr. No One drove them off Mulberry and onto Main, then stopped at a traffic light three intersections up the road. While stopped at the corner of Main and Willow streets, MacPherson saw a woman wearing sunglasses and dressed in dark slacks and a coat the color of Pepto-Bismol. She was leaning against a shopping cart half-filled with an assortment of garish garments—apparently her entire wardrobe—along with about a half dozen aluminum cans. Her short, thin hair was combed backward, like a man's. She was pointing at the car (at *him?*) and laughing like a loon.

Presently, the light changed and No One gave the Humvee some gas. As they sped past the intersection, MacPherson craned his head back until the laughing woman and buildings that surrounded her faded out of sight. In only a few more minutes, the town itself was just another distant, flickering light and all ahead of them in the windshield was blackness impaled only by the Humvee's high beams.

THE YOUNGER boy brings his own fingers to his mouth and begins to gnaw on them, nervously. He calls out, louder, to his brother. "I said, *are you okay?*" He begins to pace around this deeper-than-normal chamber into which they've fallen, his hands extended in front of him, feeling the contours of the walls, trying to gain some sense of the dimensions of the place. It's big.

Overhead, the tinkle and clang of Angels' bells grows more and more faint, beginning to asymptote toward silence. Instinctively, the boy jumps. His hands find the place where the ceiling of this lower chamber opens up. The place from whence he came. But the passage from the room above to this one below is longer than he thought. There's no way to climb up to there from here.

He falls to his knees. His voice cracks. "Angels...I'm sorry. I'm so sorry. Sorry. Sorry." He feels his nerves jangle, and like a marionette shaking on strings he cannot sit still. He paces with his hands out in front of him, muttering. "Sorry, Angels. Angels, please don't—Angels, I ask your forgiveness."

He trips. Shrieks. Flails his arms in front of him. Tumbles. There's the sound of impact against the ground. Panting. Screaming. His hands move over the darkness and find a shape lurking within it. A tube of flesh. A neck. Resting at an angle at which a neck shouldn't rest. He flinches. Shudders. Retreats back to a corner of the room. Curls up in a ball. Whispers, over and over again, "Sorry...sorry."

MACPHERSON RECOGNIZED the Quonset hut, and recognized Kitterman's face when he opened the door. Once they were all inside, the security man took time to apologize. "I'm sorry I made some misleading statements about the so-called 'background check' earlier today, MacPherson. Like I said earlier, the art isn't really my end of things."

"Oh, come now, Roger, when I saw the surveillance tape, I thought you handled yourself admirably, especially considering this had to be your first performance since...well... what...some god-awful high school play?"

"I think the last time I was on stage I was a nine-year-old shepherd at my church's annual nativity play, Mr. Krieg."

"How...bourgeois, *n'est-ce pas*, Mr. No One?"

"Well, I suppose you could say that—in any case—it was poor preparation for his present duties...both on stage and off, as it were."

"Indeed. Anyway, No One, let's get to business, shall we? Where do you plan on holding this...ceremony."

"I want a big chamber," No One said. "I want the darkness to drown us."

Kitterman spoke up. "There's a larger chamber available just a little over a mile away, in the tunnels. In Level Minus One. At least, earlier today it was there...I'm not sure if the workers already changed it."

"That new, deeper level," Krieg said. "Would that be suitable for your purposes?"

"Indeed it would. The deeper, the darker, the better."

Krieg grinned. "Then, my friend, you shall have the deepest and darkest chamber Nowhere can furnish. I want you to have access to the perfect setting, the perfect magickal accessories, the perfect props, the perfect ambiance. I want you not to

47

have any excuse to fall back on when the ritual fails and the world keeps chugging on with cruel insistence. I don't want you to be able to say, 'Alas, if I only I 'ad me Scepter of Mithras, then all would 'ave gone to plan!' or 'I didn't wear me trusty Ring of Galzabadar, that made all the difference!' or 'The bloody room was too small to 'ouse all the energy needed for the ritual.'"

Mr. No One rolled his eyes. "Is *that* what I sound like to you? You think I talk like Mary fucking Poppins?"

MacPherson yawned.

"Tut-tut," Krieg said. "None of that. Kitterman, get this"— he paused and looked at MacPherson's sweatpants and loafers— "*gentleman* some coffee, posthaste. I don't want No One to be able to make the case that the audience was too tired to fully attend to the performance, and that that's the reason why the ritual didn't work."

"Oh," MacPherson said. "That's okay. Honestly, I'm able to stay awake without it."

Kitterman poured coffee from a stale pot into a mug and presented it to Krieg. Krieg thrust it toward MacPherson. "Please," Krieg said. "I insist."

MacPherson took a sip. It tasted like mud and metal. Instead of making him more alert, it gave him vertigo.

THERE'S THE walls, there's the dark, there's the *him*. There's the wreckage of his brother's body just a few feet away. There's the walls, there's the dark, there's the *him*.

He's sitting, and begins to rock back and forth, over and over, to self-soothe. He has offended the Angels, and this is the awful penalty. Worst of all, they didn't kill *him*. They got his innocent brother instead. His brother, who believed in them all along and tried his best to bring him into the fold.

The ground is cold beneath him, and he feels vulnerable. The blackness once felt familiar. Yes, he thought he remembered light. Yearned to see it again, but he nonetheless felt at home here in the dark. Now it is as though the blackness—his home for all these years—has turned against him. He imagines the Ocean of Darkness all around him teems with avenging Angels. He rests his head against the cold ground and imagines there are creatures crawling through the soil, toward him. Hunting him down. The fall should have killed *him*, too. But it didn't. And now there are Things silently trotting and flying and crawling and slithering through the blackness, all on a mission to eat him. Or maybe the blackness is nothing more than the gaping maw of a single gigantic predator and he is falling into the gullet, in slow motion. Falling. That's what he's doing. The ground beneath him might seem sturdy but it is an illusion. Sturdiness proved to be a false assumption before. The ground, it is Nothing.

Go ahead, he thinks. *Stop toying with me and take me. The fall should have taken me. Take me. Take me quick. Don't make me suffer.*

His prayer is answered by silence, interrupted only by the sound of his pulse in his ears.

"I THINK I might be able to stand now," MacPherson said. He hugged Kitterman's office chair. From the dark tint of the room, it seemed as though he was wearing sunglasses indoors. But when he tried to rub his eyes, he found no shades there.

A bipedal thing with a long black toothy gatorlike snout spoke in a muffled voice, with an English accent. "You better not 'ave given 'im too much, Krieg. Remember, art isn't *art* without the audience." There was a ringing in MacPherson's ears before and after it spoke.

Krieg took off his beret and began whirling it around his finger. He had a veiny bald head that rotated in a tight circle as his eyes tracked the spinning hat. "How was I supposed to know he was such a lightweight? World traveler, art connoisseur. Ha! Bourgeois ninny, more like it!"

MacPherson opened his mouth to protest, but found he could only drool. The ringing in his ears worsened, too. Now it occurred even when other people were talking, not just in the silences in between.

"If you don't mind me saying so, Krieg, you sound just as obnoxious on the potion as you were before you took it. If I were a suspicious man, I'd say you might 'ave skimped on it to sabotage the ritual. No sign of sedation. Need I remind you, *all* participants need to assume an altered state of consciousness to facilitate the Great Dark Mouth assuming its Greater Consciousness over *all* of us, and then the rest of 'umanity."

"And if you don't mind *me* saying so, *you're* every bit as whacked on this souped-up LSD as you were before you took it."

"You 'ave it all wrong, Krieg. For starters, it's not LSD. It's me own special concoction. A little bit of opioid to constrict the pupils, a little bit of barbiturate to calm the nerves, and me own special, secret ingredient to open the door to Dark-consciousness."

"Yeah. Whatever. You sound nutty of course, but you're not slurring your speech or acting goofy in any other way. If *I* were a suspicious man, I'd say you might have tricked me and not, in fact, taken the potion at all...so that you could have the advantage. Maybe that was really just skunky coffee in your mug, so you could dope *us* all up and convince us later on this ritual of yours almost worked. And while I'm at it...that costume. Black robe and cheesy black mask. You look like a black reptile dressed up as a nun. Sister Godzilla!"

"Godzilla was green. Rather like the shade of Mac-*Pher*-son's skin, actually. Anyway, I *do* feel calm and mellow. Perhaps there's no change in me mental status because me mind is already quite open to Dark-consciousness. And as for your quip about me so-called 'costume'—I'm dressed in these vestments so I can consecrate the Great Dark Mouth into me very body. The vestments, the drug, the eclipse, the ritual, the prayers to Darkness tattooed on me skin. All these things are the gunpowder. Nowhere, Indiana, shall be the spark."

"Then let's get out of here," Krieg said. "What time is it anyway?"

MacPherson searched for his cell phone so he could answer that question, but remembered it was still up in his room.

Now Kitterman's voice. Off to the side, someplace MacPherson couldn't see. The sound…weak. Almost too quiet to rise above the ringing in his ears. "It's three a.m., gentlemen. If this is the night we're going to do this, then perhaps we ought to drive out to the tunnels."

"There's no ifs about it," the Black Gator Thing said. "Tonight's the night it must 'appen."

"Then let's go," Kitterman said.

"Let's?" the Black Gator Thing said. "As in 'let us'? As in Kitterman's joining us, too? I won't allow it, not until 'e takes the elixir."

Krieg stopped whirling his beret, averted his eyes from it altogether, and looked up at the Black Gator Thing. "He doesn't have to enter your ritual space. He's just going to be the chauffeur. Time's too short to walk out there, and I don't trust any of the rest of us to drive." Then he started whirling his beret on his finger again. "You got the heat-sensing goggles, Kit-Kit?"

"They're already packed in the Humvee."

"No need to pack any for me," Black Gator said. "If I'm to

52

manifest the Great Dark Mouth, then I mustn't chase away the darkness by any means. When we go underground, someone will need to guide me. Someone, preferably, besides that ass'ole with the beret."

"Um, I suppose I can be helpful in that regard?" Kitterman said, as though he was asking Krieg's permission.

Krieg kept looking at the spinning beret, but smirked. "How cute! Now No One will have a six-foot, redneck seeing-eye-dog!" Krieg affected an exaggerated Hoosier drawl. "I cain't say I know a lot about art. That thar art, t'aint muh side of the business. But I sure as hell am good to shepherd a nutty nihilist around in the dark so he can do that thar ritual, I reckon!"

MacPherson began to cough. Then retch.

"See what effect your jokes 'ave on people?"

Then Kitterman again. "Gentlemen...if we're going to conduct Mr. No One's ritual at the appointed time, then I suggest we move."

Krieg stopped twirling his beret. Poked his head up. Seemed a little less manic. A little more businesslike. "That's right! That's right! We can't give No One any excuses! Let's go. Let's see him and his nihilist principles fail. Let's see sadism emerge as superior! Oh, this is the most fun I've had in Nowhere for a long, long time!"

THIS IS the end and he knows it. He hungers, but he hears not even the slightest, distant tinkle of Angels' bells. He hears only the sound of his own too-fast breathing, and wishes it away. Now that his brother's dead, he finds the very sound of his own breath to be a blasphemy.

Something in the darkness agrees with him. It is cold and distant, but coming closer.

Somehow trotting and flying and crawling and slithering toward him, all at the same time. It is different than him. It's different from him or his brother or any of the other boys. It's different from the Angels. It's just *different.* It's bigger than him, too. So much bigger than any of the big people he's ever known. And it's coming. For him, but not *just* for him. Somehow, it's coming for the world.

He wonders if this is Judgment Day.

He wants to die. He doesn't want to wait for The Thing That is Coming. He tries to imagine what death will be like. He's so sorry about disbelieving. He believes in Angels and Heaven now. *Knows* now, for certain, he's never before seen light. His memories were mistaken. His brother was right. Was right. Now dead. His brother shouldn't have died. *He* should have died. *He* was the nonbeliever.

He tries to remain hopeful that death will bring him into Heaven's light. By admitting his sins and giving up his life, he's showing he's more obedient now. No longer a know-it-all. This must count for something with Heaven. Won't it?

But what if it doesn't. The teachers never talked a lot about Hell, they just said there *was* one. The only thing he could figure, for sure, was that Hell wouldn't have Angels in it. No Angels meant no food. So Hell was a place where you would starve.

Then the terrible thought struck him: maybe he was already there.

Trotting and flying and crawling and slithering. Trotting and flying and crawling and slithering. And walking.

Footsteps. Overhead. Voices. "Careful, No One, you're going to trip over that robe!"

Voices, and something falling down the hole in the ceiling. "Rope ladder's secured. Who will be the first one down there?"

MACPHERSON DIDN'T care to be the first to climb down the rope ladder. On an ordinary night, he would have been all gung-ho about such a venture. This, after all, was a chance to really *live*. To have an *Experience*. To get his hands dirty in the appreciation of art. But even with his heat-sensing goggles on, he didn't like the idea of climbing down without someone below to hold it steady. Maybe he was getting a little old for this sort of thing.

But at least the nausea and dizziness had passed, and these had been the worst parts. His ears still rang though. And he had these flashes. Visions. Emaciated horses, pockmarked by big black sores, galloping over an Indiana pasture. The sores grew bigger and bigger until they were like a dozen tiny mouths swallowing each animal. Then the crows, spiders, and snakes. Flying, crawling, and slithering toward him. He hadn't been able to brace himself for such hallucinations. Hadn't known he was taking a drug until it was too late. It had been too long since he'd last taken drugs. This particular light-headedness, these particular visions—so foreign. This new dope...so much more potent! It made the stuff he took in the '60s seem so tame.

Krieg got on his belly and looked down the hole. He whispered, "MacPherson, you've gotta see this!"

"See what?" MacPherson whispered back.

"Two kids. One dead. Looks like the other's on his way to dyin'."

This had been what MacPherson had traveled so far to see. Somehow, his trip to Nowhere, Indiana, had been hijacked by Mr. No One and his crackpot theories about magick, art, and nothingness. Somehow, MacPherson's special tour had become overshadowed by the impending ritual. Now, finally, here was an opportunity to let his eyes linger on the suffering he'd so anticipated. He joined Krieg on the ground to take a gander.

MacPherson had seen broken necks before, of course. One tended to see quite a lot of them while perusing public hangings in the more chaotic parts of the world. Nothing special there. Yes, there was an overall gauntness to the dead boy's body. His ribs stuck out spectacularly...but this was not exactly unexpected. He'd seen plenty such sights in Romania during the early '90s. Hell, if you got off on seeing hunger, all you had to do is watch a couple of Holocaust documentaries. But the boy who still lived...now *that* was something to behold.

The lad appeared to have started to go insane. He was rocking back and forth. Nowhere, Indiana, had utter control over every muscle in his rag-adorned body, and undoubtedly every neuron firing in his little brain as well. If there was such a thing as a soul, then Nowhere had control of it, too. And that, MacPherson decided, had been where Krieg had outdone himself. The prisoners in Beirut may have suffered highly inventive tortures of the flesh, but they could always dissociate. They could always make their minds go back to better times.

With Nowhere, Indiana, Krieg had created a world of his own... had placed children in there at such a young age they probably couldn't remember anything else. He created their entire frame of reference, created their Heaven and Hell and Angels. Krieg had long ago acquired power over life and death, but he now had power over hope and despair. Perhaps even over sanity and madness. He was, in a way, the creator of a new branch in human evolution—Wild Children of the Dark. Krieg, through behavioral art, had transcended simple sadism. Krieg had now become a sadistic god.

"I'd like photographs," MacPherson whispered. "There has to be a night-vision camera around here someplace, maybe back in the Quonset hut, right?"

"No pictures," Krieg whispered back. "Sorry. I'm sure you understand."

MacPherson nodded. He *did* understand. They probably didn't have time to go back and get a camera. Moreover, Krieg obviously didn't want stills of Nowhere floating around on the Internet. Then there was the matter of reverence. MacPherson felt that Nowhere might be just too *holy* a sight to photograph.

Then Kitterman's voice whispering. "There's kids down there? Already? The hole's pretty new. Didn't think anyone would find it already."

Then Mr.-No-One-Dressed-likea-Black-Gator chimed in with *his* muffled whispers. "What's going on down there? Why the delay?"

"Kids in the chamber," Kitterman said.

"Are you daft! They're not drugged. Their consciousness will throw off the entire ritual. Their energy will be—"

Krieg got up off the floor. "Calm down, No One. Jesus Christ. Just *listen* for a second. I don't think you have to worry that much about their goddamned *energy.* One of them's so low on *energy* his goddamned neck is broken. The other one looks like he's almost starved. They aren't going to throw off anything."

"We need to cancel the ritual. It won't work this way. I won't be able to invoke the Great Dark Mouth unless everyone in attendance submits their consciousness to the consciousness of the ritual."

Krieg jabbed a finger into Mr. No One's chest. "Stop...freaking...out. Kitterman will handle it. We'll have him go down and fetch the kiddos out of there, and then you'll have your ritual space."

"Kitterman can't go down there! He's not drugged. He's not *pure*. Send Mac-*Pher*-son instead. And don't touch the vestments! They must be kept immaculate for the Mouth!" Perhaps trying to compensate for the muffled voice under the mask, Mr. No One had spoken too loudly.

"Who's up there?" came the trembling voice from the chamber below. "Are you Angels?"

"I-I'M AN Angel," a voice calls out from up above before letting out a cough. "I've come to take you out of there."

If this is Judgment Day, is he being given a second chance? A pleasant thought, but something isn't right. He hasn't heard this Angel's voice before. He's never before heard Angels cough. "If you're an Angel, then how come I don't hear your bells?"

There's a long pause above. Then whispering. Perhaps more than one Angel up there?

"I'm just an apprentice-Angel. I haven't earned them yet. But I need to come down and get you out of there."

"My brother's dead."

"We'll take him out of there, too. But first let's worry about you. We dropped a ladder down there for you. A rope ladder for you to climb up. Do I need to come down there to fetch you or are you strong enough to use it?"

He is strong enough. It's weird. He's never felt anything in his hands like the texture of this thing that's been dropped down the hole for him to climb up. It's both firm and shaky at the same time. When his foot finds a step, it yanks the whole thing down and makes it crooked, and he has to flail his hands around to find the next step. In the end he stops trying to step up the thing—too many failures, too easy to get tripped up—and relies on his hands alone.

And then he's out of there. He feels the shifting of various presences around the hole as he emerges. They make room for him, but still seem to surround him.

He calls out to the Angel. Falls down to his knees in penitence. "Thank you for rescuing me. I promise I'll never blaspheme again. Is there any chance…any chance at all…that I may have manna?"

Another voice speaks. Not the first Angel who dropped down the climbing-thing, but another. "No more manna," he said. "No more manna, ever again. I suggest you go and try to find others of your kind. Pass on the news to them. The Angels will never bring any manna, ever again."

He kneels there, incredulous. Angels bring food. That is Reality. That has been Reality for a very long time. To say otherwise is like saying there's no ground under your feet, or no walls towering over you. To say otherwise is to say it's all coming to an end.

One of the Angels grabs him by the wrist. "Now go! I command you. Run! Go tell the others what I have told you."

What choice does he have but to leave his brother's body behind? What choice does he have but to obey?

"NO MORE manna?" Mr. No One said under his black gator mask. "I don't recall that subject coming up in our meetings."

"I wasn't making it up," Kitterman said. "I told him that because those were my instructions from Mr. Krieg."

"Maybe," Krieg said, "I don't have to keep you informed of every detail of my plans, No One."

"That's not being a good collaborator."

"Maybe not, but it is being a good artist. And who said you were really my collaborator? Maybe you're just another member of my audience." He chuckled. "Maybe you're just another of my art supplies."

"Maybe I'm just your cash cow."

Krieg sighed. "How unkind! Do you really think I'd be down here at three in the morning, indulging you in this little ritual, if I was just interested in you for your money? Seriously, if I just needed money, I'd milk a sap like the Good Mr. MacPherson down there."

MacPherson didn't care for Krieg's insults, but he didn't say anything. He was having too much fun. The body down the hole wasn't cold, the way he'd expected it to be. When he found this to be the case, he'd put his head down to the lad's chest and heard something hammering. When he'd found *this* to be the case, he put his ear down next to the lad's mouth and heard the faintest whiff of breath. The boy was wrong. His brother wasn't dead. Only *half*-dead. How *delicious*.

That's when MacPherson started to sweat. Tremble. Started to lick his lips. That's when he stared up at the hole to make certain no one was looking. He'd never before had such an opportunity. He put his wrinkled hand over the youth's soft lips. He took his other hand and pinched the youth's nostrils together. He doubted the boy could hear anything, but just in case he whispered this: "We haven't much time. You'll need to go quickly." He took a deep, appreciative sigh. "But not *too* quickly."

THE ANGEL had appointed him to be a Prophet of Doom, and he dares not argue with Angels. When he doesn't find any of the others by walking, he begins to jog. When he still doesn't run into any others, he begins to scream.

"No manna anymore. The Angels have spoken. No more bells! No more food! No more bells! No more food!"

A distant voice echoes against the walls. "You lie," he thinks it says. "You lie!"

"MACPHERSON! WE don't have all day. You're not down there diddling the corpse now, are you?"

MacPherson gulped. His spine quivered. The magic moment had passed. It made the whole trip worth it. But he'd not say a word about it to Krieg. He had the feeling Krieg wouldn't like it if he crossed the line from audience to artist, especially if he borrowed his art supplies.

MacPherson craned his head up to the top of the hole. "I've just been trying to plan a way to get him up out of here. I don't think I can lift him all the way out of here on that rope ladder."

"You should go down and 'elp him."

"It's almost four a.m. now," Kitterman said. "The peak of the eclipse is *at* four. I don't think you'll have time to move him."

"And do we really need to move him, No One?" Krieg asked. "I mean, your issue is with having a consciousness in the room that's not an *altered* consciousness. The dead kid doesn't have a consciousness at all. I don't know what all your fuss is about."

"I just 'ad a feeling. Call it intuition. Something didn't feel quite right. I thought 'e 'ad to move 'im. But now that intuition's gone. A funny thing, really. Something's changed down there since Mac-*Pher*-son went down."

Then Kitterman's voice again.

"You gentlemen really don't have the time to discuss this further."

"If we'd brought hacksaws," Krieg said, "we could just bring him up here one piece at a time."

"No time for that either," Kitterman said.

"You can put the kid down now, MacPherson," Krieg said. "We'll just leave him down there. A corpse should at least give the place a little ambiance. Now, no more table-setting, let's go down and do this."

"Very well then," Kitterman said. "I suppose I'll stand guard up here? Make sure no other whippersnappers stumble onto this place?"

"Works for me," Krieg said. "No One, you want to go down there first? That way I can help you get started down the ladder?"

"I'm not going to need a bloody ladder," No One said.

MacPherson thought he heard the flapping of wings. Then another image flashed through his brain: a crow with a piece of torn flesh in its beak, swooping down to land on a barren landscape. Then the crow wasn't the crow anymore, but it was Mr. No One—in his black vestments and black gator mask, right there in front of him.

"Let the magick begin," No One said. "Already, the Great Dark Mouth is becoming incarnate within me!"

"Looks like the drug's getting a second wind," Krieg said. "It looked like you just..."

"Get down 'ere, Krieg. This is the appointed time."

"Hey, listen. I might be letting you run this ritual, but *I* run Nowhere. Show a little respect."

MacPherson trembled as Mr. No One raised his head like a

baying wolf and roared. "Get. Down. 'ere."

Krieg started climbing down. "You really ought to be mindful of who you piss off, No One. I don't care how big a temper tantrum you have, I could still make your life pretty miserable."

Mr. No One growled at him.

MacPherson didn't care for the tension between them. Tried to diffuse it. Approached them. "So is this the part where we join hands in a circle?"

Krieg let out a laugh. "That money didn't buy you much in the way of brains, did it, dipshit? There's only three of us. The best we could form is a triangle."

"We don't 'old 'ands," Mr. No One said. His voice grew more gravelly. It didn't sound like No One anymore. It sounded like No One after twenty years of smoking. "One 'olds 'ands in a ceremony if one is attempting a magickal act that would be considered, in alchemical terms, to be one of *coagula*—that is, of putting things together. Invoking the Great Dark Mouth is just the opposite. It is an act of *solve*—which is to say, dissolution. Invoking the Great Dark Mouth is an act of taking things apart...be they the bonds between molecules or the bonds between family members. Therefore, we are to stand as far apart as possible. This is one reason why it is preferable to 'ave a large room. Krieg and Mac-*Pher*-son...I want both of you to go to different edges of the chamber, while I stand in the middle of it."

MacPherson went to the end of the chamber closest to the dead boy. No, not just the dead boy, *the boy he killed.* He liked looking at him. If the ceremony got boring, it'd give him something to do.

"Now, take off your heat-sensing goggles," No One said. "To invoke the Dark we must eschew all implements of vision."

MacPherson had forgotten No One had mentioned this before. Alas, he wouldn't be able to look at his trophy. He removed his goggles and felt, for the first time in Nowhere, real trepidation at being bathed in total darkness. The absence of light was absolute. The dark seemed bigger than him. Bigger even than Krieg or Mr. No One. Bigger than all three of them put together, bigger than their lives and plans and loves and hates. The dark seemed to soar over him and crawl under him and slither around him and gallop through him. The darkness seemed hungry for him, but not *just* him.

It occurred to him then, perhaps for the first time, that Mr. No One just might be right and Krieg (his idol, his hero) might be wrong. This was an uncomfortable thought he tried to push out of his brain, but couldn't. How surprising, that the supremacy of sadism (a belief MacPherson had been invested in for three decades) could be questioned by spending just a few hours with Mr. No One. Krieg would've undoubtedly been horrified if he'd found this out. In spite of their collaboration on Nowhere, it seemed pretty clear that Krieg saw Mr. No One as a competitor.

That was the funny thing: on one level, Krieg and Mr. No One were just two artists embroiled in a battle of egos. In this way, they were scarcely different than any other two creative types he'd ever known. But at another level, their conflict transcended ego altogether. Despite his protestations that he was just following market forces, it seemed abundantly clear that Krieg had an actual artistic *devotion* to sadism. How else could one explain the way he'd transformed *life itself* into a torture for the Wild Children of Darkness? And who in their right mind would argue that Mr. No One was anything but a true believer in nihilism? So committed was he to that cause that he gave up his own name and poured what was undoubtedly a small fortune into Nowhere, Indiana, so that it might be rendered even more unpredictable than before. So that it could become like a living creature, in and of itself. A Great Dark Mouth that would consume them all as an appetizer and the universe as a main course.

"Now, gentlemen, 'ave you removed your goggles?"

"Of course I have," Krieg said. "I'm playing along, fair and square."

"I have, too," MacPherson said.

"Very well, then our ceremony shall begin."

He clapped his hands three times. His vestments rustled. His voice now boomed. "Great Dark Mouth! Blessed Jaws of Doom who dost rise out of Nothingness to make us and our world one with Nothingness. I 'umbly do beseech thee to take possession of me, thy most 'umble servant. Enter me so that Thou might enter the plane of existence. Enter the plane of existence so that Thou might consume it. Remove, Great Dark Mouth, the Three Masks of Existence. Remove the Mask of Light, reveal the Dark underneath! Remove the Mask of Life, reveal the Cold underneath! Remove the Mask of Meaning, reveal the Nothingness underneath!

"Now we raise up to you the six-said chant: 'Remove. Reveal. Remove. Reveal. Remove. Reveal. Remove. Reveal. Remove. Reveal. Remove. Reveal.'"

MacPherson joined in. Each time he said "Reveal" he drew in a breath, and each time he said "Remove" he let one out. And so the chant began to synchronize with his own respiration. In this way, the magick began to feel much more tangible. Much more *real*. No longer did it sound like the mumblings of an English madman. Now the ritual had a home in his lungs, and he felt a coldness in his chest as the magick began to make itself at home there.

"We invite your four avatars: the serpents and stallions and spiders and crows. Let them slither and gallop and crawl and soar over us. And again, for the second time, we raise up to you the six-said chant: 'Remove. Reveal. Remove. Reveal. Remove. Reveal. Remove. Reveal. Remove. Reveal. Remove. Reveal.'"

MacPherson heard snorting and whinnying behind him.

How could this be? He had his back up against a wall. He dared not let his hand wander back there. MacPherson felt the itch of a dry, cold mane against his neck and puff after puff of cold air against his cheek. He began to think of running, then remembered that he'd have to find the ladder in the pitch-black chamber if he were to have anywhere to run to. The ladder and the escape hole were in the middle of the room—near Mr. No One. He'd have to make it past him to get up there.

All he could do was hope that Krieg was right. All he could do was hope Mr. No One was insane, and that the whinnies and snorts were just hallucinations. That the drugs he'd been slipped had somehow resurged in their potency. And so this was the direction in which he shoved his thoughts.

I'm just high, he thought. *None of this is real. It's no more real than a movie or a book. Just a story my head is conjuring at the suggestion of certain words said by Mr. No One. Just a story my head has no resistance against thanks to the work of the drug.*

"We invoke the names given you by our forebears in magick. We invoke the name Kuk. We invoke the name Erebus. We invoke the name Azathoth. Let the power of these names flow into this chamber. Let the power of these names flow through us. Let the power of these names bring 'unger to the Great Dark Mouth. And again, for the third time, we raise up to you the six-said chant: 'Remove. Reveal. Remove. Reveal.

Remove. Reveal. Remove. Reveal. Remove. Reveal. Remove. Reveal.'"

MacPherson said the words. He was terrified of what would happen if he didn't. He thought he heard Krieg say them, too. What must he be thinking of all this? Was he worried, too? Was he feeling the same sensation of something crawling up his leg? Did he hear the same sound of fluttering wings overhead?

MacPherson began to wonder if he shouldn't ask No One to stop it. Perhaps he could say he needed to use the restroom. Surely, No One wouldn't want him pissing on himself throughout the ceremony.

Then again, maybe that's *exactly* what he wanted. To frighten him—to frighten both him *and* Krieg—to frighten them to the point of humiliating them.

"We invite you, Great Dark Mouth, into our very consciousness. Let the figments we believe to construct Reality be your first feast. Feast on our figments, and leave behind only shadows! Eat our consciousness, and leave behind only fever dreams! And again, for the fourth time, we raise up to you the six-said chant: 'Remove. Reveal. Remove. Reveal. Remove. Reveal. Remove. Reveal. Remove. Reveal. Remove. Reveal.'"

MacPherson didn't want to say the words, because increasingly they were beginning to take hold. His brain was boiling from the heat of magick. He began, once again, to feel vertigo. He fell, but did not seem to hit the ground. He vomited, but had the sense that *he* was vomit, too. The Great Dark Mouth was eating the construct he'd previous considered to be his mind, and his body was being coughed up like a bit of chicken bone or a crab shell accidentally swallowed.

The Beast was now here. The Feast, now begun.

"We invite you, Great Dark Mouth, to animate the hallways of Nowhere. We reconsecrate this Temple of Suffering to you, the God of Nothingness. To you, the one true God. March triumphant through these hallways, take possession of them, and use the mere figment of suffering as fuel for your conquest. And again, for the *fifth* time, we raise up to you the six-said chant: 'Remove. Reveal. Remove. Reveal. Remove. Reveal. Remove. Reveal. Remove. Reveal. Remove. Reveal.'"

Now there was nothing but falling and blackness. And even the words "falling" and "blackness" seemed to be fading from MacPherson's awareness, seemed to be losing their meaning. All words were now like foreign ones. Jumbles of symbols. Down.

Dark. Down. Dark. Sick. Sick. Sick. Sound. The sound of Krieg barking something. Then a mechanical whirring.

Light.

Light, and the trance begins, slowly, to fade. He sees Krieg and he sees Mr. No One and he sees them gesturing angrily at each other.

Light. He *sees* light. But he still *feels* the Presence of the Great Dark Mouth.

SOMEWHERE IN the marrow of his bones, he knows the role of a prophet is a lonely one. He knows the truth he tells is so terrible that none of the other boys will want to believe it. Somehow, instinctively, he knows no other boy will ever want to join forces with him now. No other boy will step into that role vacated by his brother. But an Angel commanded him to take on this assignment, and this gives it meaning. And meaning is the fuel that makes his legs run and his heart pump. He may not have food or water or companionship, but he has a command from an Angel. Who else can say the same?

So he persists. He continues to scream warnings about the end of things: the end of manna and the end of bells. And then he hears a buzzing. And then the world is different. Something stabs his eyes. Did he keep running and running into a different world? There are things looming high on either side of him. He knocks his hand against one and hears the distinctive wood-and-metal sound.

The walls.

He looks down at the filthy hand that hit the wall. Looks at the long, chipped nails. Looks at the tiny cuts and bruises. *My hand.*

Light.

He begins to ponder. Is this what he thought he remembered from before? What he'd yearned for? It burns. He cowers. Puts his hands over his eyes. Too bright. Too bright.

Why must it intrude *now*? He wishes someone would make it
go away.

THE LIGHTS went on and Krieg was giggling and Mr. No One
was tearing off his vestments and mask and running over with
his fists clenched and Kitterman came down the rope ladder
and took a gun out of his ankle holster and pulled it on Mr. No
One.

"Did you really think," Krieg said, "I'd let you foist your
primitive superstitions here in *my* exhibit? Did you really
think that fucking home brew you concocted would disable
me? I did 'shrooms in the '70s that took me on harsher trips
than that! Did you really think I'd let you declare the victory of
nihilism over sadism, right here in *my* exhibit? You're not only
crazy, No One, you're gullible as all hell."

"You 'ad fucking *lights* installed?" He looked up and saw the
bright bulbs on the ceiling. "Installed and fucking *concealed*."

"Just over top of a retractable, false ceiling. I owe you
thanks, by the way. I wouldn't have been able to afford it
without your funding. You see, *this* is the actual artistic activity
I wanted Mr. MacPherson to come and see. The triumph of
sadism over nihilism! What do you think of this artistic
endeavor, MacPherson?"

MacPherson felt cold sweat trickle down his forehead.
Words began to reattach themselves to his brain, but he hadn't
yet regained the use of them. The Presence still lingered It

was looking at him now, out of the eyeholes of Mr. No One's discarded mask. There were shadows inside of there, and he knew the Great Dark Mouth had retreated into them. It was watching him. Watching to see if MacPherson would betray it by siding with Krieg. MacPherson looked at the mask until it was too horrible to look at, and then covered his eyes. He said nothing.

"Oh dear, it seems like all of this has shaken up MacPherson. Alas, let's hope he snaps out of it. You see, he's been the witness to it all. He'll be the man who spreads news of your defeat to all the other connoisseurs of behavioral art! I'll ask him to tell the story far and wide, of the night sadism triumphed over nihilism, perhaps because nihilism was represented by the dumbest of champions!"

Mr. No One looked at Kitterman. "This 'as all been an interestin' night now, 'adn't it? But you really don't want to use that gun, now, do you, Kitterman? I mean, you're up to your elbows in trouble already, with 'elpin' the little fellow in the beret torture kids all of these years. Do you really want to add cold-blooded murder to the list of your offenses?"

Krieg grinned his eroded-teeth grin. "This is *rich*. The so-called nihilist begging for his life! Making appeals to morality. 'Cold-blooded murder,' indeed. '...the list of offenses.' Ha! That's the sign of your final defeat...your retreat into hypocrisy. Even *you* don't believe your own propaganda! Shoot him, Kitterman. But not in the head or the chest or the stomach. Shoot him, if you can, in the kneecaps. Make him *suffer.* Make him bleed."

Mr. No One took two steps toward Kitterman. "Put down the gun, man. If Krieg wants to shoot me, then let 'im do it 'imself, you know? Remember the contempt 'e showed for you not that long ago? The way 'e mocked you? Is 'e really worth shooting a man for?"

Mr. No One was just about four feet in front of him. He had his arms extended out in front of him, making the distance even closer. MacPherson thought he looked like Frankenstein marching out of the laboratory, that way.

"Now, Kitterman. Shoot him fucking now!"

Shots rang out. MacPherson had never before appreciated how *mechanical* the act of firing a gun was. A click of trigger, a pump from the barrel. The propulsion. Then blood and bone, of course. But what made an impression on him, at least initially, were the shots themselves. Three of them. Mr. No One fell to the ground. Kitterman stood over him. "My wife has cancer and we're uninsured, fuckwad! We need the money so I'll shoot whoever the hell Mr. Krieg tells me to shoot."

The scene unfolded with Krieg kicking Mr. No One in the ribs and Kitterman whipping out a pair of handcuffs. Before tonight, MacPherson would have looked upon this with interest. He would have listened intently to Krieg's explanation of Mr. No One's fate. As it was, he felt distracted. The Great Dark Mouth still watched him, from out of the eyeholes of the mask.

He heard Krieg mumble something about leaving Mr. No One there, crippled and in the bright light, to starve along with the Wild Children of Darkness. But he didn't care about any of that. So while they were all busy, screaming and scratching and flailing against one another, MacPherson grabbed Mr. No One's discarded vestments and mask. And, when he'd climbed to the very top of the rope ladder, he put them on.

HE HEARS three sudden, loud noises and jumps. Then he sees the bright light and he winces. He jogs a few feet away and curls up against the wall. *How I wish I were just this wall,* the boy says to himself. *If I were just this wall, then I wouldn't need food. I wouldn't have eyes that could get hurt by the light. I wouldn't be a prophet if I were just a wall.*

He thinks this for a very long time. Mutters prayers that the Angels will take the burden of eating and seeing and prophesying away from him. "Just make me a wall," he says. "Please, just make me a wall."

He hears a rustling and the clipclop of footsteps. Opens a gap in between his fingers, so he can see— but not see too much. It is a Thing in Black. It has a head that isn't like his. It has big teeth. It's coming toward him.

"I've heard your prayer," a muffled voice says. "I cannot make you a wall, but I can bring back the dark."

The boy's heart races in his chest. A question's resting on his lips, waiting to be spoken—but he is not sure he has the courage to speak it. Finally, he spits it out. "A-are you an Angel?" The Black-Toothy-Thing laughs. "Better than an Angel," it says. "I am God. You wish to be delivered from sight and light, is this true?"

The boy hesitates. Trembles. Then nods.

"Then I shall deliver you from it. Let me see your eyes."

And God puts Its hands over his eyes, and there's a jumbling around, and in a matter of moments all's black.

"There, now that was painless, wasn't it?"

The boy nods and smiles, thankful for the blessing of darkness.

The sun hung high overhead when MacPherson came to, and the wind whipped his back like a scourge. He was sweaty and, with those penny loafers on, his feet ached more than they'd ever ached before. How long had he been walking? He vaguely recognized the landscape. Behind him, an expanse of pasture. Ahead of him, the small town. He must have begun walking in this direction, from Nowhere. But why? What could possibly be left for him here? What could possibly be left for him anywhere? He had the sense that nonexistence awaited him in those crumbling small-town sidewalks, and he had a sense he'd welcome it.

A gust came along and scooted him forward, almost

involuntarily. A gust like something in a hurricane, even though it was sunny. Yesterday he would have found this strange, but today his threshold for "strange" had been elevated to such a height that the freakish weather seemed positively mundane.

It was hot and he couldn't breathe well. He had the mask on. He had the robes on, which flapped madly against him in the gale. And he had something squishy clinched in each fist. He looked down. Opened his right hand slowly, *carefully*, so the wind wouldn't steal away what he had. He saw a glob of white flesh with red and pink tendrils trailing from it. He opened his left hand and saw the same, only this one was positioned in such a way that an iris was visible. Brown. With a contracted black pupil. He didn't want them in his hands.

Even more importantly, the Great Dark Mouth inside of him didn't want them in his hands. It wanted them someplace else. He lifted the mask just enough to slip the flesh past his lips, onto his tongue. When he swallowed, it was like the Holy Communion he'd last taken as a teenager. It was, admittedly, an imperfect comparison. The flesh he was eating wasn't the flesh of God. But still, the act of consuming the lad's eyeballs would make him one with the Reality of Blackness. He would become, perhaps for only a moment, an incarnation of the Great Dark Mouth. And then, if the Great Dark Mouth had an ounce of anything like mercy, it would devour him, too.

As he approached the town, cars passed. Bystanders slowed

and gawked. He didn't bother gawking back. More walking. More aching. More grunting and sweating and *being*. How he wanted to shed them all. There were a few cars parked on Main Street. One or two people strolling across it, on some errand or other. Apparently undaunted by the high winds. Doing something they imagined had some purpose. They noticed him, too. One stared. The other seemed to try to pretend she hadn't seen him.

When he reached the corner of Main and Willow streets, MacPherson saw a woman wearing sunglasses and dressed in dark slacks and a coat the color of Pepto-Bismol. She was leaning against a shopping cart half-filled with an assortment of garish garments—apparently her entire wardrobe—along with about a half dozen aluminum cans. Her short, thin hair was combed backward, like a man's. She was pointing at him and laughing like a loon.

He stopped in front of her. "You know things, don't you?" he said.

She nodded and laughed.

"This is the end, isn't it?"

She nodded and laughed.

"Then so be it."

And then the vertigo came again. A sense of shrinking and falling, shrinking and falling and *tumbling* through gulfs of cold, empty space. Perception and certainties and words and past and present and up and down and left and right and here and there all gobbled up until there was nothing left.

THE CACKLING old lady looked at her latest find, nodding and laughing, nodding and laughing. Oh, how it seemed like it had been meant for her—the way it drifted over the sidewalk and gutter and right toward her on the gentle breeze! Oh, what fun to hoard the world's junk! She'd use the robe for a light blanket on autumn nights. The perfectly good papier-mâché mask lay a few feet away from it, dented but still wearable. She'd go down to the pawn store and hock it. It wouldn't be worth much, maybe five bucks. Enough to treat herself to a small cheeseburger and drink at McDonald's.

This is how she lived—off refuse. She cobbled together an existence this way. And oh, how good, how very, very good the world was to her, to give her all the *somethings* in her cart for *nothing*. She nodded and laughed. Yes, the world was plentiful with blessings.

NICOLE CUSHING

ABOUT THE AUTHOR

NICOLE CUSHING is the Bram Stoker Award® winning author of *Mr. Suicide* and a two-time nominee for the Shirley Jackson Award. Various reviewers have described her work as "brutal", "cerebral", "transgressive", "taboo", "groundbreaking" and "mind-bending". *This Is Horror* has said that she is "quickly becoming a household name for horror fans". She has also garnered praise from Jack Ketchum, *Rue Morgue*, Thomas Ligotti, John Skipp, S.T. Joshi, Poppy Z. Brite, Ray Garton, *Famous Monsters of Filmland*, and *Ain't It Cool News*. An Italian translation of *Mr. Suicide* (titled *Mister Suicidio*) was recently published by Independent Legions Publishing. A native of Maryland, Nicole lives with her husband in Indiana.

ACKNOWLEDGEMENTS

Children of No One was the first book I wrote that included several references to the occult, and this challenged me with a steep learning curve. I'd like to thank Nathan Drake Schoonover for assisting my research by sharing his knowledge of magick in general and Theyyam rituals, in particular. I'm also indebted to the work of Alejandro Jodorowsky and Alan Moore, who have both enriched my understanding of the powerful connections between ritual and art.

Thanks to Todd Manning for his work as a beta reader, and to Joe Pulver and W.H. Pugmire for their encouragement.

Thanks to Alessandro Manzetti of Independent Legions Publishing for rescuing this book from out-of-print oblivion. Thanks to Lucy A. Snyder for editing this new edition.

Last, but not least, I'd like to acknowledge my husband for always loving me unconditionally and supporting my writing ambitions (even when they become obsessions). I think I'm gonna keep him.

CHILDREN OF NO ONE

FORTHCOMING BOOKS

THE BEAUTY OF DEATH 2 – DEATH BY WATER
Anthology – **Paperback and eBook Edition**
Edited by Alessandro Manzetti and Jodi Renée Lester
October 2017

DREAMS THE RAGMAN
by Dennis Etchison
Novella – **eBook Edition**
October 2017

TALKING IN THE DARK
by Dennis Etchison
Collection – **eBook Edition**
December 2017

AVAILABLE BOOKS

THE RAIN DANCERS
by Greg F. Gifune
Novella – **eBook Edition**
September 2017

THE WISH MECHANICS
by Daniel Braum
Collection – **Paperback and eBook Edition**
July 2017

THE ONE THAT COMES BEFORE
by Livia Llewellyn
Novella – **Paperback and eBook Edition**
May 2017

SELECTED STORIES
by Nate Southard
Collection – **Paperback and eBook Edition**
April 2017

THE CARP-FACED BOY AND OTHER TALES
by Thersa Matsuura
Collection – **Paperback and eBook Edition**
February 2017

ALL-AMERICAN HORROR OF THE 21ST CENTURY
Edited by MortCastle
Anthology – **Paperback and eBook Edition**
November 2016

BENEATH THE NIGHT
by Greg F. Gifune
Novel & Novella – **Paperback Edition**
October 2016

THE BEAUTY OF DEATH
Edited by Alessandro Manzetti
Anthology – **eBook Edition**
July 2016

DOCTOR BRITE
by Poppy Z. Brite
Collection – **eBook Edition**
January 2017

WHAT WE FOUND IN THE WOODS
by Shane McKenzie
Collection – **eBook Edition**
September 2016

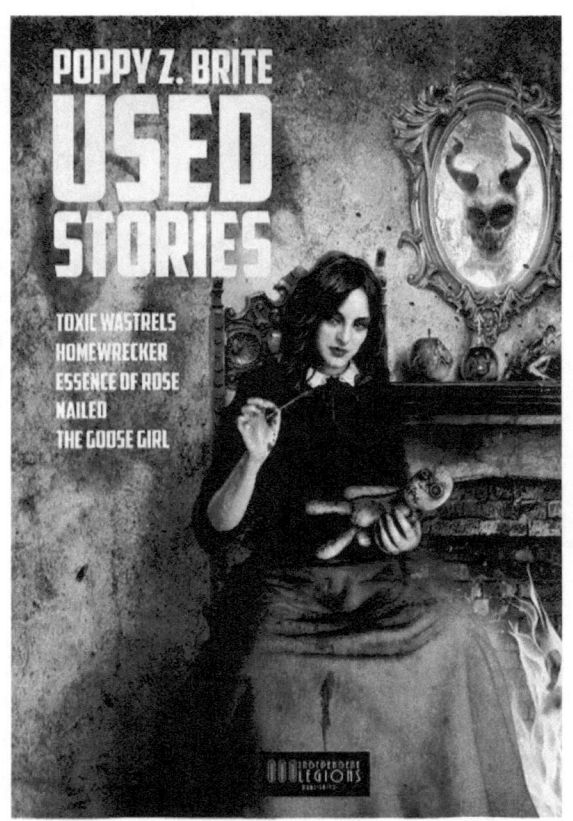

USED STORIES
by Poppy Z. Brite
Collection – **eBook Edition**
June 2016

THE HORROR SHOW
by Poppy Z. Brite
Collection – **eBook Edition**
August 2016

SELECTED STORIES
by Edward Lee
Collection – **eBook Edition**
July 2016

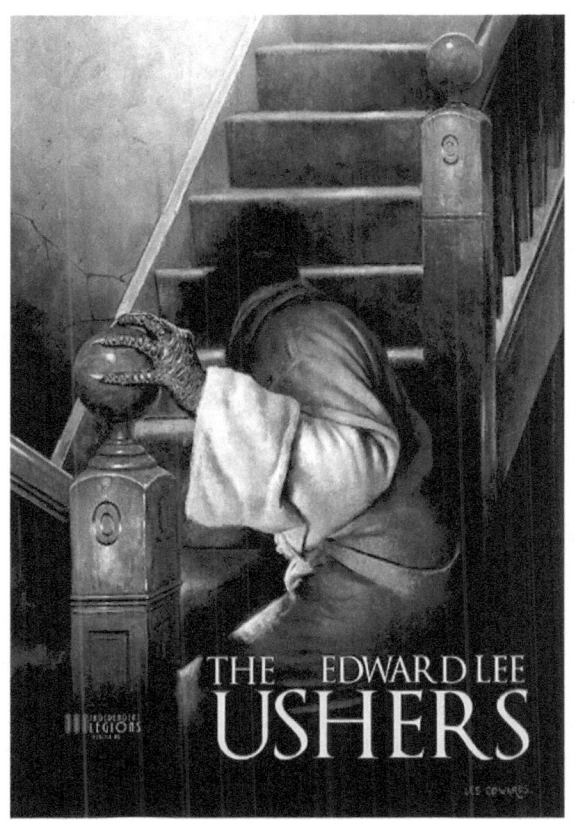

THE USHERS
by Edward Lee
Collection – **eBook Edition**
May 2016

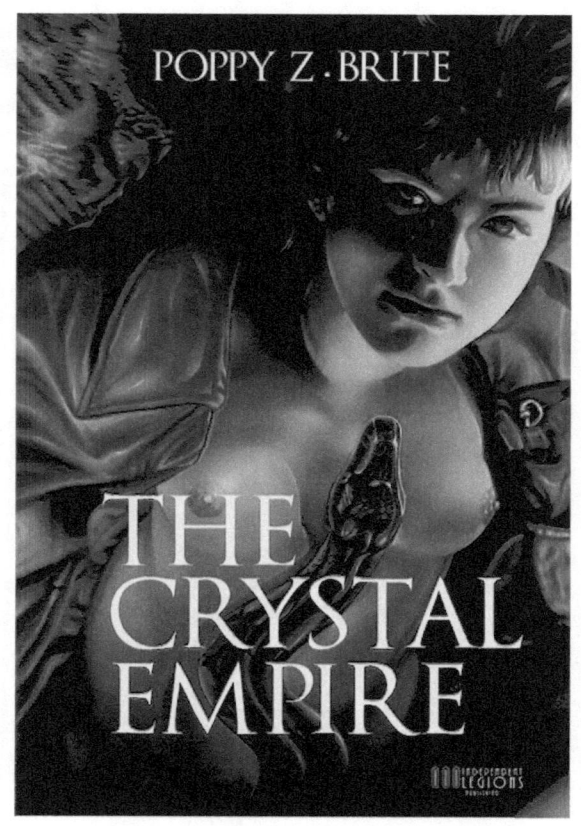

THE CRYSTAL EMPIRE
by Poppy Z. Brite
Novella – **eBook Edition**
May 2016

SELECTED STORIES
by Poppy Z. Brite
Collection – **eBook Edition**
February 2016

THE HITCHHIKING EFFECT
by Gene O'Neill
Collection – **eBook Edition**
February 2016

SONGS FOR THE LOST
by Alexander Zelenyj
Collection – **eBook Edition**
April 201

INDEPENDENT LEGIONS PUBLISHING
di Alessandro Manzetti
Via Virgilio, 10 - 34134 Trieste (Italy)
+39 040 9776602

www.independentlegions.com
www.facebook.com/independentlegions
independent.legions@aol.com

Books in Italian:
www.independentlegions.com/pubblicazioni.html

www.ingramcontent.com/pod-product-compliance
Lightning Source LLC
Chambersburg PA
CBHW022040170626
46808CB00003B/1296